FINAL GRAVITY

A TROUBLE BREWING COLLECTION

LAYLA REYNE

Final Gravity

Cover Design: Temptation Creations

Editing: Susie Selva, Sandy Bennett

Second Edition

December 2025

E-Book ISBN: 978-1-962010-58-0

Paperback ISBN: 978-1-962010-56-6

Content Warnings: Explicit sex; explicit language; instances and/or discussion of homophobia.

ABOUT THIS BOOK

Good trouble.

Dominic Price & Cameron Byrne
were supposed to get married
a year and a half ago.
Their family and friends
request the honor of your presence
at their wedding,
which shall not be further delayed.
Period.
For details, contact Agent Lauren Hall,
chief instigator who is tired of waiting.

Nic & Cam get married, plus newly added extra scenes in this Trouble Brewing special collection. Final Gravity and the additional scenes in this collection should be read after the other books in the Trouble Brewing series.

GRAVITY CRAFT BREWERY
REDWOOD CITY, CA · EST. 2013
TROUBLE BREWING · LAYLAREYNE.COM

UNFAIRLY GOOD

March 2018
(During Blended Whiskey - Agents Irish & Whiskey 4.5)

Nic's beer was unfairly good.

And so was the prosecutor himself.

In the way he'd put aside whatever lingering awkwardness still existed between him and Jamie to be here for Aidan today, same as he'd been there for all of them the past year through one roller coaster after another.

In the way he looked in that light gray suit and silvery blue tie, the monochromatic fabric making his eyes glow icy blue.

In the way he argued in a courtroom or with Cam about their cases, beer, or sports teams, their back-and-forth exhilarating—and seductive, even now as Nic argued him into a corner with the uncomfortable truth no New England Patriots fan ever wanted to admit.

Certainly not one as devoted as Cam.

"I'm sorry?" Nic said, hand cupped around his ear for

dramatic effect. Rubbing it in. His gotcha smirk was as attractive as it was infuriating. "I didn't hear your answer."

Cam forced it out through gritted teeth. "None."

"Right, none," Nic said. "And Brady lost to who? Oh, that's right, twice to Eli Fucking Manning and once to a fucking backup." He looked unfairly good even taunting him with his arms spread wide, pretending to be a fucking bird. "Fly, Eagles, Fly."

Or maybe that was just the beer and whiskey talking to Cam.

Definitely his dick.

In any event, he needed to stop Nic from talking. And there was something he was unfairly good at too.

Turnabout was fair play.

"Is that the Manning Face you're—"

Two strides across the elevator and there was no more talk about football, quarterbacks, or birds. He grabbed Nic's chin and put his mouth to better use, prying open his lips and plunging his tongue between them.

And *fuck*, why did he have to taste good too?

Cam's favorite beer combined with a taste that was uniquely Nic, that with one swipe of his tongue Cam knew he'd never be able to shake from his senses. Just like the groan that rumbled from somewhere deep in Nic's chest, a sound straight out of Cam's fantasies.

Wanting more of those sounds, wanting his senses overwhelmed by Dominic Price, he shoved him back against the elevator's mirrored wall and dove deeper, exploring every corner of his mouth, every new flavor and every wanton moan that reverberated around his tongue.

Every inch of Nic's hard body pressed against his.

Arguing hotter than they ever had before.

And because Nic was better at arguing than anyone Cam

had ever met, he effortlessly turned the tables—making Cam melt with his hands in his hair, his tongue thrusting into his mouth, his dick grinding through layers of material against his.

Owning him.

Because Nic was that fucking good.

Cam contemplated shoving down their pants and taking their dicks in hand together, the only opening he had for winning this argument, but before he got the chance, the elevator dinged.

A forced time-out.

He ripped his mouth from Nic's, gasping for breath and grasping for words. A lick of his lips, the taste of Nic and his beer still on him, brought a threatening few to mind. "If you ever accuse me of having Manning Face again, I swear I will turn a keg of your best beer green."

Nic's blue eyes danced with heat and amusement, a devastating combination. Distracted, Cam barely heard his words— "I believe this is your floor, Agent Byrne"—and left himself vulnerable to the former SEAL's maneuvers. In a blink, Nic was behind him, palming a handful of his ass before shoving him out the door. "Later, Boston."

Cam could play the torture game too, grinning over his shoulder and adjusting his aching dick without an ounce of shame. "Sooner, Price."

In his fantasies, as soon as he got back into his room.

In reality before long, that kiss winning the motion and moving their case to trial. Cam couldn't wait to argue with the prosecutor some more.

A HERESY OF PUMPKINS

October 2018
(Between Craft Brew and Noble Hops)

"What the fuck are you doing?"

Cam glanced up from the pumpkin he was carving to meet the fiery blue eyes of his boyfriend. "What's it look like I'm doing?"

Nic tossed his coat and tie on the only table not covered in newspaper and pumpkin goo and proceeded to *stalk*—only word for it—across the room. "It looks like you're making a fucking mess of my tasting area."

Hands by his side, Cam shook them off onto the newspaper on the floor behind the bar that Nic couldn't see. Then almost laughed out loud as Nic turned a brighter shade of red. "Better watch it, Counselor. You're starting to look like your boss."

Nic cut his gaze to the nearest pile of seeds and string,

fingers twitching, mind making a calculation Cam was sure would go his way.

Which it did.

Nic bypassed the pumpkin ammunition, not willing to subject his precious tasting room to further collateral damage. He stopped on the other side of the bar, unbuttoned his collar and sleeves, then braced his hands on the outer edge of the bar top, arms spread wide. He looked good, if a bit wrinkled and worn out. Bowers had been riding him hard since they'd returned from Boston, as if the week away on a case that had led to multiple other case closures had somehow been a vacation.

"This is why you left work early?" Nic asked, eyeing the gutted pumpkins on the bar.

"I left work early to help decorate." Cam gestured around the tasting area that he, Eddie, Steph, and Ang had decked out for Gravity's Halloween Party tomorrow night. Alternating skull and pumpkin lights were strung wall to wall, the tables under the newspaper had fall-themed Gravity slicks on them, and all the taps had new ghoulish tap heads.

Nic, however, remained fixated on the pumpkins, smartly assessing the most dangerous threat in the room. "And these are part of those decorations?"

Cam nodded, keeping the details thin and stoking the fire in Nic's eyes. He really shouldn't bait him, it had been a long week, but Cam couldn't help it. The reward would be so worth it.

"Why are there five?" Nic said.

Cam strolled down the back bar aisle, laying a hand on each tap as he passed. "One, two, three, four, five."

Nic's brow furrowed. "Not following, Boston. Spell it out for me."

"How about I show you?" he said with a wink.

He reached under the bar and pulled out one of the screw taps he'd laid on the shelf there. After screwing it into the hole he'd carved in the middle pumpkin's side, he turned it around to face Nic.

The horrified gasp echoed around the cavernous room. "You didn't."

Cam shrugged, eyes wide, playing dumb. "Didn't do what?"

"Do you not remember the conversation we had at Aidan and Jamie's wedding?"

"About green beer. I remember." He grabbed a glass and drew off a pint of Nic's favorite, the Palo Alto Pils. "Something about being dead to you . . ." Grinning, he moved to pour the pilsner into the tapped pumpkin.

Nic caught his raised arm by the wrist, stopping him short. "If you love me, you'll rethink your next move."

"But I'm doing it because I love you." He tipped the glass and poured the beer into the pumpkin.

"I'll show you love," Nic growled before vaulting over the bar the next instant. The instant after that, the glass was tossed in the sink and Cam was tossed over his shoulder. Nic slapped his ass, hard enough to sting and just right for revving Cam's dick to full attention. "Dead to me."

"After you fuck me, right?" Being honest, that's what Cam had been after all along. "On your desk."

"The desk, the chair, the floor, the truck, then our bed. Five places, five hard fucks, for those five acts of heresy on my bar. Your ass will be dead when I'm done with it."

Cam mentally added the kitchen table, for when Nic found the sixth pumpkin keg at home, full of imperial stout.

VALENTINE'S INK

February 2019
(Before the last scene of Noble Hops)

Nic didn't fidget. Aside from a tendency to drum his thumbs when he was thinking, the prosecutor moved with efficiency. Or didn't move, sometimes going eerily still. The SEAL beneath the attorney's pinstripes.

Unwinding all that pent-up efficiency—getting his boyfriend loose under his hands and mouth—was one of Cam's favorite things. But pliant with lust was a far cry from the man squirming across the table from him. All of Cam's investigative instincts were pinging. Not with worry; they were past the point of hiding from each other. If Nic were injured, or if this were something major, he'd have told Cam. This was something else, and the unknown made Cam more curious than ever.

"Ants in your pants, Counselor?"

Nic glanced up from the chocolate soufflé they were

supposed to be sharing. He'd drawn it closer to his side of the table, bite by bite. Setting aside his spoon, he shifted in his seat again and grumbled, "That's about what it feels like."

Cam tried not to choke on his rye whiskey. "Explain."

"I'd rather show you."

Cam coughed and sputtered, struggling to swallow the fiery alcohol. "Can I guess what this is about?"

"Can you get the check?" Nic countered. "We've got a limited time window."

"Then why the fuck have you fidgeted through a two-hour dinner?"

"Boston."

"Dominic."

"Because it's Valentine's Day, and you deserved it." Nic pushed the heart-shaped soufflé dish to the middle of the table. "You deserved more of this too. We'll come back next week and get you your own."

If it wasn't indecent to crawl under the table and blow his boyfriend, Cam would. He flagged down the server instead. Five minutes later they had the check. Ten minutes after that, Cam was swinging the truck into their driveway. Not a lot of time to pry out more details.

Aside from the fidgeting, the only other clue was a brown paper bag Nic pulled from the center console. But even that clue wasn't much help. Nondescript, no odors, and folded over as it was in Nic's grip, there was no room for whatever was inside to rattle around. If it even rattled. In any event, it wouldn't be lube. Cam had that on subscription.

Bird was also interested in the mystery bag, sniffing it as Nic bent to give him a hello scratch. "Not a treat for you, Joe."

Smiling, Cam shut the front door and leaned back against it. "Maybe the name change would stick if there really were treats in there."

"Ignore him, Joe." Nic gave him one last scratch before disappearing down the hallway.

Bird *meowed* miserably, used to more attention from his favorite. Cam scooped up the furry traitor and tickled his belly. "I don't know what's going on either."

"Get back here," Nic shouted from the bedroom, "and I'll show you."

The paper bag crinkled, as if Nic was balling it up, and Bird wriggled to get free. "I don't think so, buddy," Cam said. "That bat signal's for me." He wrestled the cat into the study with a toy, then kicked himself into high gear, shedding layers as he made his way to the bedroom.

He was down to his undershirt and pants when his step faltered in the doorway. A day didn't go by that Cam wasn't struck by the cypress tree tattoo on Nic's back. Once a symbol of the past Nic had run from—a past Cam had worried might threaten their future—it had come to represent something good since last fall. Survival and a family found. Everything Nic deserved, and Cam was honored to share it with him.

Moving the rest of the way into the room, Cam stepped behind Nic. He coasted his hands up the cypress's knotted trunk and splayed out his fingers as he traced its spindly branches. A shiver snaked through Nic's tall, trim frame, and his belt buckle *clacked* as he fumbled undoing it. Grinning, Cam peeked around Nic's shoulder. His smile died at seeing the supplies scattered on a towel on the bed. Bandages, medical tape, and first aid ointment. He clasped Nic's shoulders. "Are you hurt?"

"Far from it." Nic shoved his pants and boxers down, and the heavy belt buckle took them the rest of the way to the floor, revealing the last piece of the puzzle.

A bandage over Nic's left hip. Where Nic's hand so often drifted. Where he'd told Cam he intended to ink a certain drawing. A new memorial to join the others on his skin. This one to Cam.

Whipping around, Cam grabbed Nic's wallet off the dresser and riffled through the billfold. Last fall, in a seaside motel, when Cam had feared he was on the verge of losing Nic, his boyfriend had pulled out a sheet of well-creased yellow legal paper and shown Cam the rough sketch of a tattoo. One that symbolized their future together.

Cam dropped the wallet back on the dresser. The sheet of paper was gone. But it wasn't really. It'd just been made permanent. "Is that what I think it is?" he asked.

Nic grinned over his shoulder, both sly and shy. "Happy Valentine's Day, Boston."

Cam laid a hand over the bandage and for the first time tonight, Nic settled, letting out a relieved sigh. "Feel better?" Cam asked.

"Pressure helps the itch."

Cam applied a little more. "When did you do this?"

"That continuing legal ed class I was supposedly in all-day… Well, it wasn't."

"Can I see it?"

"That's the limited time window part." Nic shifted, hip turned toward Cam. "It's already going to be red and swollen, and it'll only get worse as it heals. This is your last chance for a few weeks."

Cam nodded, words locked up in excitement and emotion.

Nic began peeling back the medical tape that secured the bandage but only got one corner free before he curled his fingers as if to itch.

Cam knocked his hand away. "Maybe I better do this." He took over, murmuring apologies as Nic winced and hissed. The bandage fluttered to the floor less than a minute later.

Nic was right. The area on his outside left hip was angry

and glistening with salve but the design was visible. Every detail Cam remembered from that rough sketch was there on Nic's hip, brought to vivid life. His fingers floated on air above the tattoo, tracing the design. A play on the label for Gravity's forthcoming FBI Stout, except the tattoo had a red BoSox styled B, in place of the brewery's falling apricot, as the top leaf of a green Celtic clover.

Him—them—forever inked on Nic's skin.

Christ.

"What do you think?" Nic asked, voice rough.

When Cam didn't answer—couldn't answer—Nic slid his fingers under his chin and tilted up his face. Only then did Cam realize he'd knelt to take a closer look. His eyes flickered back to the tattoo, unable to tear his eyes away. "I don't… I can't… Baby, I…"

How did one put words to the abject wonder that made his head spin? To the colossal, comforting weight of appreciation and love that made his heart explode? To the lust that made his dick hard as rock?

"You, speechless." Nic chuckled. "Now that's a rare sight."

Normally, he'd shoot Nic a glare for the sass, but Cam was still too entranced by the tattoo and all it stood for. "Never seen a sight like this."

Nic hauled him up by the shoulders, and Cam stared into blue eyes fiery with emotion, reflecting everything Cam also felt. As did the kiss Nic laid on him then. Nothing held back, all of his gratitude, love and desire there for Cam to taste.

"You like?" Nic asked between kisses, same as he had that night in Gravity when they'd first tasted the FBI Stout.

Cam's answer was unchanged. "Yes, I fucking like." Drawing back, he lifted a hand and cupped Nic's cheek, the gray-flecked stubble there tickling his fingertips. He rested his other hand atop Nic's hip, above the tattoo, then slid it back and down, palming Nic's ass. "It's gorgeous. You're gorgeous. How'd I get this lucky?"

"I'm the lucky one." Nic stole another quick kiss before reaching for the supplies on the bed. He held them out to Cam. "Help me put the bandage back on?"

Nic walked him through the process—dabbing the inked area clean, then applying the salve, bandage, and tape. After, he handed him the towel with a soft "thank you."

"I get to do this, every night," Cam said.

"You don't have—"

"You did this for me." He set the towel and supplies on the dresser. "Let me do this for you."

"I did this for us."

Nic drew him back into his arms and into another deep, claiming kiss. Cam savored the heady brew. The mingling of dark chocolate and spicy bourbon, the jumble of teeth, lips and tongue, the blend of now and forever. Until Nic's left hand drifted lower... to scratch his hip.

"No you don't," Cam chided, slapping it away again.

"Sorry, those ants I mentioned early."

"Except your pants are gone." Laughing, Cam flopped onto the bed and shimmied out of his own slacks. "And now mine are too." He rid himself of the rest of his clothes and scooted over, making room. "How'd you survive all the rest?" he asked, eyeing Nic's decorated torso.

"It's been awhile." Nic lowered himself onto his right side, facing Cam. "I have to remember to slap, not itch." He brought his hand down in a light slap atop the bandage. "The pressure and sting distract."

"Distract." Cam hummed, distracted himself by an idea that had suddenly and powerfully taken hold. He inched closer, bringing them chest to chest, and nudged a thigh between Nic's legs. "Like this?" He mimicked Nic's slap, fingers hitting the bandage with light pressure.

It had the desired effect. Distraction of a different sort. Nic gasped and his cock hardened where it was pressed against Cam.

"Or like this?" He brought his hand down again, harder and farther back. His palm met round, firm ass cheek and pinpricks of heat radiated down Cam's fingers. And straight to his cock.

Nic's voice was tight and gravely when he spoke. "That's a spank, Boston."

"I know." Cam pressed his thigh against the underside of Nic's balls and rolled his hips, rutting his aching cock against Nic's. "Are you distracted?"

Icy blue eyes burned into his. "Again."

Cam didn't need to be told twice. Alternating between light slaps to the bandage and heavier smacks to Nic's ass, Cam quickly reduced them to a moaning, writhing mess. Nic half-panting, half-begging "Again," and Cam thrusting harder and faster against him, until the friction wasn't enough. Nic rolled onto all fours and Cam moved behind him, more desperate than ever to get inside him. Nothing he or they had ever done before had been this hot. But it wasn't just the spanking. Or the new tattoo. Or the heat of Nic's ass cheek pressed to Cam's pelvis as he drove into him. It was the trust, the love, this man, their bed, and everything they were building, together. Which was also how they came, together. A final slap, a ragged scream, and Nic's red, trembling ass clenching around Cam as he buried himself to the hilt inside the man he loved.

When Nic's limbs began to wobble, Cam tipped them sideways, falling the rest of their way onto their right sides. Curled around Nic from behind, Cam laid one hand over his heart, and the other over the bandage. "That distract you for a bit?"

"For a bit." Nic snuggled his ass firmly into the cradle of Cam's hips and put a hand over Cam's, over the tattoo. He tangled their fingers, let out a sleepy satisfied sigh, and finally stilled. "Love you, Boston."

Cam kissed the back of his shoulder. "Love you too, Dominic." He followed his boyfriend into sleep, his heart and future secure in his arms.

FINAL GRAVITY

SEPTEMBER 2020

ONE

Dominic Price worked hard. Federal prosecutor. Liaison between the Northern District of California's US Attorney's Office and San Francisco's FBI field office. Co-owner of Gravity Craft Brewery.

Professionally, as Assistant Special Agent in Charge of said FBI office, Cameron Byrne witnessed the first two daily, riding into the Federal Building with Nic each morning and frequently working cases together. Personally, as Nic's fiancé, he just as frequently witnessed the brewery owner, the two of them spending much of their spare time at Gravity. Evenings, weekends, and sometimes in the middle of the night if this or that pressure sensor went off and Nic's phone woke them with an alert.

Today was one of those days when Cam understood just how hard Nic worked at his side hustle. With Gravity co-owner, Eddie, called out on an emergency Coast Guard operation, Nic was managing Gravity's fall release solo. Sure, the brewery had two assistant managers and multiple other staff, but they were all busy setting up the event area and back lot for tonight's food truck rally. A weekend ritual at Gravity, it would be more packed than usual tonight with the new release. Which left Cam and Nic with their hands full in the warehouse—tracking inventory, moving boxes, shifting pallets, and loading crates for each distributor, shipper, or restaurant that pulled up to the loading dock.

It was a day full of hard physical labor. And unintended foreplay that cranked Cam's sexual frustration to the max. Stolen seconds eyeing Nic's lean and powerful body, imagining the sway of tattoos under his snug Gravity tee. Countless minutes reveling in the pride shining from Nic's blue eyes and daydreaming of tasting the sweat that trickled from his silver-flecked temples. Too many tempting hours drowning in the scent of the person Cam loved most.

So after they packed the last shipment onto its truck, sorted the boxes in the warehouse, parked the forklift, and retreated to Nic's office—where Nic practically fell into his worn leather chair—Cam fell to his knees in front of him, determined to exact revenge for the hours of torture and reward them both for the day of hard work.

"Cam, what—"

"If you have to ask what I'm doing, you're not half as smart as I thought you were." He shoved Nic's knees apart and buried his face in his groin, inhaling deep as he nipped at the inseam of Nic's jeans.

Nic groaned and his thighs trembled beneath Cam's hands. Taking advantage of the rare moment of weakness, Cam wrapped his fingers under Nic's knees and yanked him forward, sliding his ass to the edge of the chair, bringing Nic's cock even closer. Cam mouthed the growing length through the denim while teasing his taint, making Nic's moans deeper . . . and louder.

"Jesus, Boston." Nic squirmed in the chair like he couldn't decide whether to thrust up against Cam's mouth or drive down on his hand. But while his body was obviously on board for either, his mind was still protesting. Arguing was the other thing they did best, after all. "Anyone could come in."

A token protest, judging by Nic's whimper when Cam removed his hand and mouth. And besides, they'd fucked back here before—after the great pumpkin-keg incident, after Nic's proposal, at least a dozen other times over the year and a half since.

"Your co-owner is gone," Cam said as he worked the button on Nic's fly free and lowered the zipper. "And everyone else is too busy to notice the boss man missing." He pushed the denim ends aside, dipped a hand inside Nic's briefs, and pulled free his cock. "It's just us, baby."

Cam leaned in and nuzzled Nic's groin again, this time getting the full effect. Musk, sweat, Nic. He ran a tongue along the underside of Nic's cock. The taste . . . mmm . . . Even better than the FBI Stout Cam had spent all day sampling and loading onto trucks. Wanting more, he closed his lips over the tip, sucking hard and then hollowing out his cheeks as he swallowed Nic to the root.

Nic surrendered—hips tilting up, ass scooting forward, arms dangling over the armrests, head hitting the chair back. But Cam wasn't done getting his payback. He sucked up and down twice more before pulling off and sitting back on his haunches, enjoying the debauched view in front of him. "Seeing you do something else you love is almost as much of a turn-on as seeing you suited up for the courtroom."

Nic righted his head, cheeks flushed and eyes hazy with lust. "Almost?"

Cam smirked. "You wear a suit better than anyone, Counselor." He ran his hands over Nic's quivering thighs, preparing to get back to Operation Blow Their Minds, when Nic stopped him with a hand to his shoulder.

"I think I have a solution to your 'almost'?" He tilted in the chair, reaching down to open his bottom desk drawer. He rooted around inside it, then after a moment, righted himself with a metallic blue necktie in hand. Cam's favorite. Grinning, Nic draped the tie around his neck. "Better?"

Cam laughed. The tie looked ridiculous hanging over Nic's rucked-up T-shirt, but taken together with the erect dick jutting out of his jeans and the about-to-get-fucked look on his face, the whole picture was hot as hell. "I've only got one complaint," Cam said.

"Oh yeah? What's that?"

"That tie needs to be wrapped around your cock."

"Christ, the mouth on you." And from the way said cock hardened more, Nic wanted Cam's mouth back on him too.

"You like it," Cam said with a wink, then gave them both what they wanted, taking Nic's cock in his fist and guiding it back to his mouth.

"Thank fuck." Nic raked a hand through Cam's hair, grasping the sweat-dampened strands, hanging on for the ride.

Cam hummed in pleasure as he worked Nic over, setting a relentless pace, one Cam mirrored with his other hand stroking his own cock, freed from his jeans and boxers. He loved getting them off together like this. Nic's cock swelled in his mouth—he was close—which drove Cam there faster too.

Nic bucked up. "Fuck, I'm—" His words died, and his body froze.

Except not in the about-to-come way.

Click-clack, click-clack, click-clack.

Cam had heard it in the same instant. High heels striking the brewery's cement floor, growing louder as the person walking in them approached the office. Realization dawned the next instant. He recognized that confident gait and all-too-familiar staccato rhythm.

Fuck.

He moved to stand, and Nic moved the opposite direction, rolling the chair forward, spreading his knees on either side of Cam and forcing Cam under the desk. Cam fell on his ass, the silk tie hit his face, and a split second later, the office door creaked open.

"Price," Melissa Cruz barked like she was still an FBI Special Agent in Charge. The badge was long gone, but there was no denying she still ran the show around these parts. "We have a problem."

Cam agreed. A hard dick in his face and a hard dick hanging out of his own pants, plus an unexpected visitor who was the best agent he'd ever known and was now a badass bounty hunter totaled up to a big problem. Mel cased every room she entered. Would she detect him hiding under the desk? It had a full wooden front—she couldn't see him—but could she smell him? Smell what had been about to go down in here before she'd barged in? Or would the day's sweat give them cover?

Nic had yanked down his shirt, and he answered Mel, his demeanor cool, calm, and collected. "Maybe we should take this elsewhere," he said to Mel.

Great idea, otherwise Cam wasn't getting out of the hole that was too small for his broad six-foot frame. Except how was Nic going to go anywhere with his pants undone? Cam inched forward to try to help zip him up. Nic kicked him for the effort.

Mel, however, proved a bigger problem. "On the contrary," she said. "I'm right where I need to be."

"What's going on, Cruz?" Nic said.

"One of my bounties is going to be at Gravity. Tonight." By

some grace of God, her footsteps backed away from the desk. "Meet me at the bar in five, and I'll brief you."

Cam breathed a sigh of relief.

"And bring Cam with you."

Thank fuck she couldn't see him turn fourteen shades of Irish red.

The door shut. Nic rolled his chair back and laughed out loud. "You should see your face right now, Boston."

Cam crawled out from under the desk and smacked Nic's knee. "You kicked me!"

"I was five seconds from coming. I didn't need your hands anywhere near my dick, especially with Mel in the room."

Now no one was coming. But Cam wasn't about to let Nic forget what they'd started . . . or think they wouldn't finish it later. He moved quickly, lunging forward and looping the tie around the base of Nic's dick, tying it in one of the sailor's knots he'd learned as a kid on his dad's boat. Not so tight as to cut off Nic's circulation—heaven forbid—but tight enough to keep the tie in place until Cam could take it off later, preferably with his teeth.

He sat back on his haunches, grinning. "I do like it better there."

Nic's mouth slammed down on his, tongue diving between his lips and making Cam dizzy with the want he still tasted there. "I wonder . . ." He nipped at Cam's lips. "Who's more turned on by this? Me or you?"

Cam knew the answer, but no way was he conceding this fight. At least not until later when they'd surrender together. "You'll have to wait and see." He pressed his smiling lips to Nic's. "Later, Price."

Nic's curved to match. "Sooner, Boston."

TWO

As Nic strode out of his office, he struggled not to focus on the cool silk tie ends brushing the inside of his left thigh, or on the snug fit of the sailor's knot around the base of his dick, or on what the man walking beside him had been doing to his dick five minutes ago.

"Stop thinking about the tie," Cam said, as if reading his mind.

"This is going to be the longest goddamn meeting of my life."

"And you're not even technically on the clock."

"I'd curse her if I didn't think it would rebound somehow."

Cam shook his head furiously, an amusing impression of their friend and colleague, Agent Lauren Hall. "Don't tempt fate."

At the end of the hallway, before they rounded the corner to the tasting area, Nic grasped Cam's arm and pulled him to a stop. "You don't have to stay here for this. You are off the clock."

Cam's dark eyes flared. "One"—he lifted his free hand and

gestured around them—"community property once we get married."

Nic bit back a laugh. "Not exactly how it works, and our fourth marriage license expires in five days." They kept meaning to get married. Something low-key and informal, just friends and family, probably here or at the house. Lauren and his sister, Lette, had been on their cases about it nonstop. But between trials, cases, the never-ending remodel on the house, and Gravity's busiest year to date, those ninety-day license windows seemed to expire in a blink.

"Details." Cam freed his other arm and lifted that hand too, pointing his index finger directly at Nic. "And two, you're crazy if you think I'm going to leave you here to deal with this alone. Hell, I should be sending you home. This is a law enforcement matter."

Nic stepped closer, and Cam's flailing hands landed on his chest. "You are not sidelining me from protecting my own brewery."

"Figured you'd say that." Cam slid a hand down between them, palming Nic's cock through his jeans and resurrecting the erection Nic was trying—and failing—not to focus on. "And three, I'm not leaving here tonight until I take that tie off your cock with my teeth." He tightened his grip, swallowed Nic's growl with a scorching kiss, then released him, spinning away and throwing a "Let's go, Counselor" over his shoulder.

He disappeared around the corner, and affectionate jealousy streaked through Nic. Cam could pull off that just-fucked look—whether actually the case or not—and no one would think twice. Dark tousled hair, dark eyes, a sinful smirk that lived on his face half the time already. Cam's cockiness was part of his charm. Nic didn't have that same easy charisma. He had to rely on his prosecutor's mask instead, which unfortunately wasn't always foolproof around Cam.

It needed to be today, though, with his staff and Mel just around the corner. Inhaling deep, he drew down the mask and coached down his erection before entering the tasting area. He found it both more and less deserted than expected. More in that his staff was nowhere to be seen. Everyone was outside judging by the voices and noises drifting in through the open back-lot door. Less in that Mel and Cam weren't the only people in the room. Daniel Talley, Mel's husband, stood behind the bar, pulling taps and filling pint glasses.

"Help yourself," Nic said.

Danny flashed him a devilish grin. "Don't mind if I do."

"You making the bartender gig official?" Whenever the youngest Talley was here, he always found his way behind the bar, and today he even looked the part—dressed in jeans, a Gravity tee, and a worn pair of Chucks.

"You want to tell my dad, or should I?" Danny replied. "How do you think he'll take the news? He's been loving his retirement." Danny was CEO of Talley Enterprises, his family's shipping empire, and Mel was TE's chief of security, along with running a successful bounty business on the side. Danny set another pint of FBI Stout on the bar in front of Nic. "Only way Dad would find that acceptable is if you've managed to talk my brother into taking over."

Behind them, Mel and Cam laughed out loud, and Nic couldn't suppress his own chuckle. As much as Aidan Talley loved his family, his allergy to the family business was legendary.

Four glasses in hand, Danny skirted through the open bar flip. "Guess that answers that question."

Nic followed him to the table where Danny passed beers to Mel and Cam. "So then, you're here about this bounty business too?" Nic claimed a glass and the chair next to Cam. "Or for the free beer?"

Danny's dark eyes glittered with poorly concealed mischief. "Both."

"I need a decoy," Mel said.

Said decoy dramatically swept an arm in front of himself. Mel rolled her eyes and caught her husband by the wrist, tugging Danny down into the chair beside hers.

"Should we be here?" Nic said, gesturing at himself and Cam, then toward the back lot. "Should my people and patrons? We're expecting a full house tonight for the new release."

"Which is excellent, by the way," Danny said with a tip of his glass.

"It's all by the book," Mel said, and Nic swore he heard an unspoken relatively tacked on at the end. "I'm here, getting the owner's permission"—she tilted her own glass at Nic— "and we should be able to apprehend the bounty before things really get going tonight. The food trucks arrive early, correct?"

Nic glanced at the clock over the bar. "In about an hour. We don't open to the public for two."

"You do staff dinner?" Mel asked.

"Of course."

"Good. We'll gather them in here, then execute the take-down outside."

"Are you sure your bounty will be here tonight?"

"Am I sure about the bounty I've been tracking for a month?" She leaned forward, glaring daggers across the table at him. As it was autumn, she'd traded her skirts and stilettos for cashmere, denim, and boots, but the heels on the latter were no less high. She tapped one pointy end against the floor beneath the table, a tempo for her rapidly thinning patience. "Yes, Price. I think I know what I'm doing here."

Cam stopped guzzling his beer for two seconds to interject,

"It's been a long day, Mel, and he's just worried about his people. And to be fair, we've torn this place up a time or two."

Nic raised his hands, palms out. "And to be fair," he echoed, "I was part of that destruction each time, but it never happened with civilians here. As long as we can protect everyone, I'm on board to help."

"Tell us what you've got," Cam said to Mel. "Who's your bounty?"

Seemingly appeased, she relaxed in her chair, glass in hand, and continued after a long swallow. "James Daley. Charged with grand theft auto, DUI, and property destruction." She traded her glass for her phone, tapped the screen several times, then handed the device to Cam. He tilted it so Nic could see the mugshot displayed. Daley looked like every high frat boy ever—shaggy blond hair; glassy red eyes; wrinkled designer polo; a carefree, doped-up smile, enjoying his buzz despite the circumstances, sure he'd get out of them. "Skipped bail earlier this month."

Nic ran the numbers in his head. "That bond is at least a hundred grand."

"Try two fifty," Danny said. "He jacked a Lamborghini Urus while high with his frat brothers. Fucking gorgeous car . . . until he ran it into a light pole."

Mel side-eyed her husband. "You don't need another car."

Danny hid his I'm-still-going-to-buy-one smile in his beer.

"I don't remember hearing about this," Nic said to cover his laugh.

"Local. The perp and the car," Mel said. "No one was present, first-time offense, pure smash and grab by a doped-up idiot, which is why I'm not concerned about him threatening anyone here tonight."

"But he skipped bail," Nic said, trying to make the irregular pieces fit. "A not insignificant amount either."

"His parents are wealthy. They posted his bail. He jumped it for a party aboard a private yacht and hasn't been seen since."

"How did you get the case?" Cam asked, handing the phone back to her. "Not your usual."

Cam was right. Mel tended to run down war criminals and high-profile targets, not idiot frat boys.

"His parents are relentlessly pestering Chief Kane about the whereabouts of their son."

"Probably more about the bond money," Danny mumbled.

"Probably," Mel agreed. "In any event, Kane's got enough other shit on his plate. I can take this off it, and I owe him the favor."

"How do we know Daley will be here tonight?" Nic asked, hoping the rephrasing of his earlier question would go over better.

Mel tilted her head in acknowledgment. "He fancies himself a restaurateur. A food truck he funded is making its debut here tonight. I don't think he'll miss it. And we have this . . . " She swiped her finger across the phone screen, then laid it back on the table for them to see. "That's Daley stepping off a sailboat in Carmel this morning."

Nic wasn't focused on the picture as much as on something else Mel had said. A debut food truck. "Meat & Cake?" he asked.

Cam whipped his face to the side, grin almost as goofy as Daley's in his mugshot. "Ooh, yes, please."

Nic rolled his eyes and put a hand to Cam's chest, giving him a playful shove. "It's the name of the food truck, Boston. They're the only new one on the list tonight."

"That's the one," Mel confirmed. "Flip to the next picture."

Nic swiped left across the phone screen.

"ATM caught that picture of Daley next to the food truck outside a San Jose ghost kitchen about an hour ago."

"Eddie said they checked out." Nic sank back in his chair, nestling into the warmth of the arm Cam had slung across the back. It was a much-needed comfort as Nic's worry began to grow. "I was in trial all week, so he did all the paperwork."

"They do check out," Mel said. "Legit operation. I doubt they even know who they're in business with."

"Poor guys," Danny said. "Brilliant name and concept. Maybe I'll fund them when this is all over."

She elbowed him in the side.

Nic quirked a brow. "Problem?"

"A whole list of 'em."

"Hey!" Danny squawked.

Mel ignored him and leaned forward, her confident gaze urging calm. Nic knew that look; he gave it to witnesses on the regular. "But I promise, Nic, I won't let this op be a problem for Gravity tonight."

Her promise should've made Nic feel better, but after the last few years, the worry in the back of his mind wasn't getting any smaller.

THREE

Meat & Cake was the last food truck to arrive, parking in the only available stall next to the back-lot driveway. And it was a sight to behold. Cam felt doubly bad for the chef-owners who were about to get the rug pulled out from under them. Someone had put real work into this. Freshly cleaned and shined, the truck's base coat was a glossy Carolina blue, and the prominent logo of a pink dancing pig holding a cake platter was a cheeky masterpiece. Add to that the whitewall tires, polished chrome bumpers, and hammered chrome cutouts, and it was clear this baby was someone's pride and joy. And it was going to be seized as evidence before it even got a proper debut.

"It's like Easter threw up all over my back lot," Nic groused as he drew alongside Cam just inside the warehouse door. From this vantage point, they could see the entire lot, but they wouldn't be the center of attention.

Cam backhanded Nic's abs. "Oh, come on. That logo is adorable."

"You just want to know what it smells like in there."

"I know what it smells like in there. My best friend is a pitmaster."

"Think their barbecue is better than Jamie's?"

"Probably not, but I'm not gonna let the product in there go bad if we have to seize the truck."

Nic chuckled, low and rumbly, and a shiver raced up Cam's spine, reminding him of what he'd rather be doing.

Later.

He glanced between them and over his shoulder toward the warehouse interior where staff dinner had been set up. "Everyone good?"

"Yep, and once they're done eating, I gave them a list of extra indoor checks. Should keep everyone busy and out of harm's way."

"May not take that long," Mel radioed through the comm unit tucked in Cam's ear. "Here we go."

Nic tensed beside him, having received the same message, and Cam swung his gaze back around, first to where Mel had crept out of the main building's back door, slipping behind the closest truck, then to Danny, who was pretending to be the staff member assigned to truck check-in. He approached the target's driver's side door and knocked twice on the window. The setting sun glared against the glass as it was rolled down; the person inside would be visible at any second . . .

Danny leaned against the side of the truck, blocking Cam's view. "Hi, gorgeous," he said, voice loud and clear, flirt turned up to twenty. Decoy was right. "I'm Danny. Here to check you in."

"I spoke to an Eddie on the phone," a woman replied, the tone of her voice vaguely familiar even if her accent was not. In any event, not James Daley.

"Eddie's the co-owner. Also Coast Guard, and he got a callout this morning. I work here, and besides, I'm cuter."

"Well, aren't you a charmer?"

"I like to think so."

Cam couldn't see Danny's face, but he was sure the other man had thrown in a wink.

"Just need to see your licenses and permits," Danny said. "And maybe a menu."

"Oh sure, just one sec. James, can you grab me a menu?"

"He's in there," Nic said, edging forward.

Cam shot out an arm, blocking the door and Nic's instincts. Nic's protective streak was one of the things Cam loved most about him, but even if Nic was an ex-SEAL, he wasn't the LEO in this relationship. "Hold," Cam said. "One, we need the positive ID from Danny." So far, their lookout was only flashing one finger at his side, not the two that would signal go. "And two, we're only here for backup. This is Mel's takedown." And she was already on the move, sneaking two food trucks closer to the target, only one left between her and Meat & Cake.

"Someone asked for a menu," replied a male voice in a Southie accent. Except not quite.

Same as the woman's accent, something about the man's rang as off to Southie-raised Cam. And didn't Mel say Daley's family was local? But Cam didn't have time to contemplate the inconsistencies, Danny flashing a second finger.

Go.

Mel appeared from the rear of the truck she'd slipped behind, now at the back door of Meat & Cake. She raised a fist and banged on the door. "James Daley, open up, bail enforcement."

A second later, Danny almost fell to the ground as the truck revved to life and lurched toward the driveway.

Cam dropped his arm, instantly in motion with Nic at his side as they ran out of the warehouse. As planned, they positioned themselves between the other trucks and the target, forming a perimeter, Danny falling behind them. For her part, Mel had jumped onto the bumper of the blue truck, hanging on by the chrome door handle. "Bail enforcement agent, stop!" She wrenched the door open and disappeared inside.

The truck, however, didn't stop, burning rubber and throwing up loose gravel that forced Cam and Nic to shield their eyes and turn away. By the time the dust settled, the truck was squealing out of the lot and hanging an impossible left-hand turn on two tires before landing back on all four and racing down the alley.

Danny barreled between them, sprinting after the truck. "Let's go!"

"We can't catch it on foot," Cam hollered. "We need to call this in."

"Fine, do that, but do it from my car, which is parked on the curb out back. We've got a chance at catching them in the Mas."

"We can't all fit in your Maserati," Nic said, even as he ran after Danny, leaving Cam to catch up.

"We'll make it work. They've got Mel, and right now, you two are the best shot I've got at getting my wife back."

Cam thought Mel was probably Danny's best shot at getting Mel back, but the fear and panic in the younger Talley's voice was enough to make Cam shut his trap and offer whatever support he could. Which meant, as the shortest of the three of them, pretzeling himself into the "back seat" of Danny's garish yellow sports car.

Cramped as he was, Cam struggled to get his phone out of his pocket. Danny flooring the gas and racing after the food truck didn't help, practically slinging him around in the back seat. Where was the oh-shit handle in this thing? Danny cut down streets and through neighborhoods, following the truck and confusing Cam. Where the fuck were they going? The freeway? The 280? Why, when Gravity had been less than a block from the 101?

Setting confusion momentarily aside and trusting Nic to help Danny navigate, Cam finally freed his phone. He rang Aidan first; got his voicemail. He tried Lauren next. Sure, he could have immediately called this into the local police, and he might have to if Meat & Cake—and Danny—kept breaking traffic laws, but Lauren might be able to finesse that with the locals. And as a hacker, she could tap into cameras and traffic lights to give them an advantage.

"What's up?" she answered, and Cam clicked his phone over to speaker, holding it so Nic and Danny could also hear.

"Either Mel's been kidnapped by a frat boy in a food truck," Cam said, "or she's hijacked the food truck."

"I'm betting the latter."

"It was a bounty," Danny said. "He made a break for it but not before Mel got into the—"

Nic slapped the dash, cutting him off. "Danny, that light's about to turn re—"

Danny screeched through the intersection behind the truck, horns blaring on all sides. Cam grabbed Nic's shoulder and slammed his eyes shut. Nic's hand came down on top of his, squeezing tight. Two breaths later, when no jolt off course or crunch of metal followed, and Nic's hand on top of his tightened, Cam reopened his eyes.

"Holy fuck," he cursed, digging his fingers into Nic's shoulder, confirming reality. They were really still there. And gaining on the truck.

"What just happened?" Lauren demanded.

"You don't want to know," Nic said.

"First order of business," Cam interjected. "Tap into the traffic signals on Woodside Road in Redwood City and turn all the southbound lights green. Turn all the other lights red. We need a clear path."

A flurry of keystrokes echoed over the line, then, through the windshield, Cam watched as all the traffic lights ahead of them turned green.

"Good," he said. "Now get us some backup. RWCPD units to the 280. Tell them it's an officer-involved incident."

"You sure about that?"

"Just do it." He gave her the details on Danny's car and the food truck, then hung up. Righting himself, he leaned forward between the seats as they sped toward the Alameda. Past that intersection, it would only be a mile to the 280. "We should have intercepts at the freeway."

"That enough time for them to get there?" Danny said.

"Let's fucking hope so."

Except as they sped across the Alameda and down the winding hill toward the 280, there were no sirens, and as the freeway overpass came into sight, no officers or troopers.

"Fuck, if they get on the freeway..." Cam said.

"They won't," Nic said with a shrug.

A shrug. And why the fuck did he sound so calm?

"What do you mean they won't? Where the fuck are they going?"

"Oh, I think I've got a pretty good idea."

"What are you on about?" Danny said as he tailed the truck under the freeway, heading toward Woodside.

Ignoring him, Nic shifted in his seat, turning toward Cam. "What color is that truck, Boston?"

Cam's gaze automatically flickered past Nic, out the window to the truck in front of them. "Carolina blue."

"And what's it serve?"

"Barbecue."

Why was this starting to feel like an interrogation?

"And who do you know who could drive a food truck like that?"

"Jam—"

Oh, that dirty fucking asshole.

"Exactly," Nic said as he flopped back in his bucket seat. "What was it you told me was your favorite part of visiting Jamie's family?"

"His sister's fucking red velvet cake." Cam slapped Danny's arm. "What the fuck is happening here?"

Taking his foot off the gas, Danny slowed the car and relaxed into his seat, catching Cam's eye in the rearview mirror. The determined, panicked face Mel's husband had worn the past fifteen minutes melted away, replaced by the wicked grin Danny wore most often. "Something that should have happened a long time ago."

FOUR

Nic wasn't surprised at all when Meat & Cake, now traveling at a lawful speed, turned at the stone marker for the Talley family's Woodside estate. Danny followed the food truck through the open iron gate and up the gravel drive to the front of the grand manor home. While not exactly the same, the sprawling house resembled the pictures Nic had seen of the original Talley manor in Ireland.

Nic likewise wasn't surprised when, once they'd parked and climbed out of Danny's Maserati, the back doors of Meat & Cake swung open to reveal a perfectly safe and sound Melissa Cruz . . . and a grinning Jameson "Whiskey" Walker.

What was surprising, however, was their attire. Jamie stepped down from the truck first, flipping out the tails of his tuxedo. He held out a hand for Mel, who had changed out of her boots, jeans, and sweater and into sky-high pumps and a shimmering rose-gold cocktail dress. And dangling from Mel's other hand was a garment bag branded with a local tuxedo shop's logo.

Rewinding the past twenty minutes, Nic tried to put the rest of the pieces together. Nic had experienced a Jamie Walker car chase from the passenger seat before. No one was as talented behind the wheel. And when the food truck had zoomed away from 101 toward Woodside, and when no backup had met them at 280, he'd put those two pieces together and guessed—correctly—at the ultimate where of the "chase." But the why of it had still eluded him.

Danny's words echoed in his mind. Something that should have happened a long time ago.

He fit that piece together with Mel's and Jamie's attire, the additional garment bag, the lit-up house, and the faint music he heard floating out through the stone archway that led to the house's patio and backyard.

The picture resolved, and Nic rounded on Danny, who had hung back by the car. "Is this what I think it is?"

Cam was charging the opposite direction toward his best friend. "What the fuck is this, brother?" he practically shouted at Jamie.

"A tux," Jamie said, poorly mimicking Cam's Southie accent. "With tails. Your favorite, I know." He took the bag from Mel and handed it to Cam. "A little birdie told me your fourth marriage license is five days from expiring."

A third person appeared at the doors of Meat & Cake. "That little birdie was me," Lauren said, doing a much better impression of Jamie's Southern accent. Brown hair in a styled topknot, wearing a flouncy orange dress and silver ballet flats, she hopped down from the truck. "You assholes"—a glittery nail gestured between Nic and Cam—"are getting married today. End of discussion."

"They both need a shower first," Danny added. "Thankfully, the house has ten."

"So helpful," Nic said.

Cam pivoted, his dark eyes swinging back to him. "Did you know about this?"

"Not a damn thing. It's release day at the brewery. A wedding was the last thing on my mind."

"It's been the last thing on either of your minds for a year and a half," Lauren said. "No matter how many of us pester you about it."

"And release day was the perfect cover," came another voice from the direction of the archway. Nic glanced over Cam's shoulder and was socked with another surprise. Eddie stood in the lengthening evening shadows, dressed in full military uniform.

"Was there even a Coast Guard mission today?" Nic asked.

Eddie strode toward him. "Of course not," he answered cheekily.

Nic punched his shoulder as soon as he was in range. "I don't have a tux."

"No, you don't." A tuxedoed Aidan stepped out the front door, Nic's uniform bag in one hand and Victoria, Nic's half sister's mom and his unofficial stepmother, also formally dressed, on his other arm. They descended the steps and crossed the drive to Nic. "You are a terrible fucking SEAL," Aidan said with a grin. "Aren't you always supposed to be prepared?"

"I didn't have marriage on the agenda today," Nic replied, taking the bag from him.

Detaching herself from Aidan, Victoria stretched up on her toes to kiss Nic's cheek. "Better pencil that in, sweetie." She stepped back and handed him the leather binder full of his military medals. A binder she'd secretly sent to him when he'd earned his officer stripes.

He pulled her into a hug, even with his hands full. "I'm so glad you're here." So glad she and Garrett were in his life again and his sister, Lette, too. So glad they were all here for his wedding day.

"Me too." She stepped back and wrinkled her nose playfully. "And Danny's right. You need a shower."

He didn't doubt it.

"Is that his uniform in there?" Cam piped up, his voice colored with eager anticipation, a total one-eighty from the ire of a minute ago.

"Indeed it is," Eddie said.

Nic caught his fiancé's dark gaze—the good, heated kind—and for the first time in the past half hour, Nic remembered the tie around his cock and quickly shifted the hanging bag in front of him.

Thankfully, Mel's sharp double clap drew everyone's attention her direction. "All right," she said. "Let's get this show on the road."

Everyone's attention except Cam's. He drew alongside Nic on their way inside the house. "You better put that tie back on after your shower," he whispered, reminding Nic of Cam's earlier promise. "Counts as something blue. And you also better dance with me," Cam added, reminding Nic of the promise he'd made to Cam when they'd gotten engaged.

A promise Nic looked forward to finally fulfilling tonight. He leaned in, lips brushing the shell of Cam's ear. "Later, Boston."

Cam nipped his jaw. "Sooner, Price."

FIVE

Cam had worn a tux for Aidan and Jamie's wedding, which, fittingly enough, had been the first time he'd kissed Nic. Two and a half years later, he begrudgingly donned the tails again. Small price to pay to marry the love of his life—finally—in front of their friends and family.

From his spot at the far end of the manor's courtyard, Cam looked out over the rows of chairs filled with familiar faces. All of his family had flown in, a shock he'd received when he'd stepped out of the bathroom earlier to find his three brothers in the attached bedroom—Keith in his USMC uniform and Bobby and Quinn in dark suits. His mom and dad had been downstairs, trading recipes and stories with the Talleys, a whole lot of Irish going on.

Friends and coworkers from the FBI and USAO were also in attendance—AD Moore, Jack Hayward, Matty fucking Kim, the Admiral, Tony with Abby on his arm. Plus Nic's family and all their friends. It seemed a miracle the trellis-covered courtyard held so many people and that so many people had shown up for his and Nic's wedding. How had no one let the surprise leak? They were never going to hear the end of it from Lauren.

Music started from across the courtyard, beyond where Eddie stood on "Nic's side." Glancing that direction, Cam received another shock. Two chairs had been arranged to the side, and Lette sat in one, a guitar on her lap, her currently magenta hair pulled back. None of that was a shock. Cam had come to learn that Lette played multiple instruments and changed her hair color as often as Lauren repainted her nails. The shocking part was the person who'd claimed the seat beside her—Keith—who was also playing a guitar. Since when did his brother play? And so well?

Jamie's elbow in his side snapped Cam out of his awe, and Aidan's nod toward the back of the courtyard had Cam swinging his gaze around. It snagged first on Aidan's niece, Katie, halfway up the aisle, tossing rose petals. He gave her the Mister Potato Head face that used to make her giggle and now made her roll her eyes, the look so reminiscent of her uncle that Cam laughed out loud. His laughter died, though, as his gaze skipped over her shoulder to the man several feet behind her.

It could have just as easily been Cam walking up the aisle, or they could have bypassed the aisle bit altogether, but Cam had selfishly wanted the excuse to admire Nic in his uniform. Cam patted himself on the back for his selfishness, but the mental gesture didn't carry nearly enough weight for the moment. This was a Nic that Cam had never seen before. With Victoria on one arm and Mary on the other, the two women who'd raised and protected him after his mother's death, Nic wore an expression of total peace, one that cracked his prosecutor's mask to pieces. Nic's smile was so real, so unencumbered, that Cam had to force himself not to bolt down the aisle and touch it—taste it—for himself. He wanted to share that feeling with the man he loved, so happy Nic had finally found it and so happy to witness it.

Nic was beside Cam in less than a dozen steps and the tsunami of contentment Nic brought with him walloped Cam. "You look hot as fuck," Cam whispered low. "And I don't just mean the uniform." He palmed Nic's cheek and brushed a thumb over the corner of his smile. "This is amazing."

Nic smiled wider. "You in that tux is a good look too, even though I know you hate it." He angled his face to kiss Cam's palm and a warm, gentle wave followed in the wake of the tsunami, lapping at Cam's heart.

"Worth it," he said.

Nic gave his palm one more kiss, then gathered Cam's hands in both of his. "Let's get married, Boston."

The rest of the ceremony was a blur—Aidan officially welcoming the guests, Jamie and Eddie saying a few words, Aidan leading Cam and Nic through the vows, Jamie producing a ring that matched the one Nic had given Cam when he'd proposed, Aidan pronouncing them husbands, Katie clapping and shouting "Now kiss."

Cam happily followed the little lady's order, kissing his husband to a courtyard full of cheers and, when Cam bent Nic backward, deepening the kiss, to catcalls too. Cam didn't care and neither did Nic, no objection to be heard from the attorney who tightly wrapped his arms around Cam, happily lost with him in their own world.

Until Keith and Lette began playing a Dropkick Murphys tune and the aforementioned Irish contingent—expats and Bostonians—was ready to party. It was a long half hour down the aisle, repeatedly waylaid by friends and family wanting hugs, but eventually they reached the backyard, which had been decked out for the reception—including a bar, a buffet, high and low tables, and a dance floor.

It was near a corner of the last that Cam eventually found himself, an arm around Nic's waist, one of Nic's over his shoulders, as they chatted with their closest friends. "Truth time. How did you guys pull this off?" Cam asked.

"How did you keep this a secret?" Nic translated for him.

Mel tapped a manicured nail against her champagne glass. "I threatened bodily harm if anyone cracked."

"She's not lying," Jamie mumbled into his own glass.

"And let's not forget the annual TE holiday party," Danny said. "Especially that one on the boat."

Everyone groaned, recalling that night of holiday mayhem.

Mel patted her husband's shoulder. "Don't jinx this, Daniel."

"I only meant pulling this off was easy, relatively."

"Well, thank you," Cam said.

"Truly," Nic added. "This was incredible. Thank you."

Lauren huffed, her breath fluttering her bangs. "I'm just glad I can finally delete that calendar reminder about your ever-expiring marriage licenses."

"Only one thing left to do," Aidan said as he extended an arm toward the dance floor.

Nic's arm tightened around Cam's shoulders. "You sure about this, Boston? I'm a bit rusty."

Cam handed his bottle of FBI Stout to Jamie, relieved Nic of his too, then tugged his husband onto the dance floor. "As sure as I've ever been about anything. Dance with me, Counselor."

One rusty dance, Cam leading as Nic only stepped on his toes a half dozen times, became a second less toe-crushing one, until countless dances later, they were moving together as smoothly as Lette and Keith played. They were interrupted from time to time by guests, but they always found their way back into each other's arms.

Peaceful, happy, content.

More in love than Cam had ever been with his man.

His husband.

Who he was increasingly eager to take home.

He'd gotten his dance. Now he wanted to fuck his new husband.

Shifting closer, he brought his mouth to Nic's ear. "You know the best part of having the wedding here?"

"What's that?"

"We're only ten minutes from home."

"You know what's even better . . ." Nic rubbed his jaw against Cam's, the scruff-to-scruff friction firing all of Cam's nerves. "That tie still around my dick. Waiting for you."

Cam groaned and forced himself not to jump his husband in public. Besides, he had a better idea for a fast getaway. "Good thing you just married a guy who knows how to boost cars."

Nic drew back, brow raised, one corner of his mouth twitching. "But which one for our wedding chariot?"

There was really only one choice. "Let's go boost a food truck."

SIX

Nic pinned the last of his service ribbons into the leather binder as Cam, minus his tuxedo coat, sauntered into the bedroom.

"Does Joe forgive us?" Nic asked.

"Bird," Cam corrected. He slipped the binder from Nic's hands, zipped it, and set it on the dresser. "And debatable. His dinner was hours late."

The orange ball of fluff had voiced his displeasure the second he and Cam had stumbled through the front door, meowing pitifully from his perch atop the sofa. They'd managed to detach their lips and untangle their limbs long enough for Cam to feed the cat and for Nic to text Mel, telling her they'd return the truck tomorrow and asking her to threaten bodily harm to anyone who intended to interrupt them further tonight.

Moving closer, Nic slid Cam's already loosened bowtie the rest of the way off. "Hopefully he doesn't divorce us."

"He might for parents who feed him timely and aren't confused about his name."

"Oh, I'm not confused."

Cam rolled his eyes and began unknotting Nic's tie. "I can't believe you stole my cat."

Nic trembled, the brush of Cam's knuckles against the underside of his jaw more erotic than it had any right to be. Maybe because Nic couldn't stop thinking about another knot he wanted Cam to untie.

"Well," Cam said, "he's half yours now anyway."

Nic chuckled. "That's not how community property works," he repeated for the second time that day.

Cam tugged free the tie, tossed it on the dresser, then stepped chest to chest. He could push Nic's coat off his shoulders, so slowly, so fucking tempting. "How does it work, Counselor?" he asked, his lips ghosting over Nic's throat.

Nic had to clear the gravel from his voice before speaking. "You have to commute prior owned property." Still sounded scratchy. "You have to demonstrate the intent to make the property ours."

"One, I think we belong to the cat, not vice versa. And two, I can't rip Bird in half." Cam shifted a step away to hang up the coat in their closet.

As soon as the coat was secure, Nic tugged Cam back by a belt loop, crashing his back against Nic's front. Wrapping his arms around Cam from behind, Nic ran his hands down Cam's torso, slowly, returning to the earlier torture. He began unfastening the buttons of Cam's dress shirt on his way back up. "Of course not," he said. "We can't do that."

"And I'm never conceding his name is Joe." Cam's voice was as low and rough as Nic's, both of them near panting. "But we can share feeding and litter duties."

"So generous." Nic lowered the shirt down his husband's arms with the same slow reverence Cam had used to remove his coat.

Cam's head fell back against Nic's shoulder. "Something else I'd like to share with you."

"Yeah?" Nic nuzzled behind his ear. "What's that?"

Cam tilted his ass up, nuzzling it against Nic's erection. "My cock, after I take that tie off yours and make you come."

"Fuck, Boston."

Slow left the building. Nic pitched the shirt toward the laundry with one hand and yanked Cam's undershirt up with the other, dragging it off over his head and pitching it the same direction. Cam spun in his arms, lips crashing against his, and Nic groaned down his throat, desire pouring out of him. All day he'd wanted this man—a day that had started at the brewery, included a wild car chase, and ended with them married. Finally. As a SEAL, then prosecutor, Nic had experienced more than a few adrenaline rushes in his life, but nothing compared to this day. And all that adrenaline was cresting on a wave of overwhelming joy and blinding need.

Cam must have felt it too, smiling against his lips. "Too many clothes, baby." He quickly divested Nic of his dress shirt and tee, followed by his belt, and was halfway to his knees before Nic remembered something else he needed to say, the joy he needed to share with Cam out loud. He clasped Cam's shoulder to stop his descent. "Wait!"

Cam straightened, brows knitted. "Is everything okay?"

"Everything is better than I thought it ever could be." He grasped the heated skin at Cam's waist and rested their foreheads together. "I just . . ." Warm hands glided up his chest, fingers fanning out over the myriad of tattoos, giving Nic time and keeping the fire between them warm while he gathered his words and his heart, ready to offer it up on a silver wedding platter to Cam. "I always thought we'd write our vows, but—"

Cam chuckled, the breath puffing over Nic's lips. "But our

friends hijacked our wedding." Hands cupping his neck, Cam drew him in for a quick, soft kiss. "What would you have said, Counselor?"

Nic leaned back far enough to see Cam's face and so Cam could see his. He took Cam's hands in his and lowered them against his chest. "I would have said that these past two and a half years have been the best of my life. That you are the best part of my life, and you've made all the other parts of my life better too. My brewery is better with you, my job is better with you, my family is better with you. My life is better than I thought it ever could be."

"Jesus, Nic."

"You, Boston, make me better."

Using Nic's hands in his, Cam yanked him forward into a scorching kiss. When they came up for air again, after they'd fumbled out of the rest of their clothes and stumbled back to the bed, Cam stood between Nic's spread legs. In what was perhaps the most surprising thing of the day to Nic, Cam ignored the tie-wrapped cock straining his direction. Instead, he framed Nic's face with his hands, and Nic smiled, cheeks lifting and lips curving, chasing more of the gentle, loving touch.

Cam's thumbs skated over his cheekbones. "I'm glad I broke the rules for you, Dominic. Every single one of them was worth it to end up right here, with you, in our life together. Thank you for always being the rope I needed, thank you for always tugging me back to shore, and thank you for not mentioning Tom Brady once today."

Nic covered the lump in his throat, the sting behind his eyes, with a watery laugh. "It was really fucking hard."

"I'm sure it was." One corner of Cam's smile hitched higher. He smirked as he lowered a hand off Nic's face, skirting it down between them, over Nic's neck, his chest, and around his belly button, a trail of sparks in its wake. A path that caught fire as Cam finally seized one of the silk tie ends and gave it a tug. "But let's focus on something else that's hard instead."

Moaning, Nic held himself upright by sheer force of will, which began to crumble when Cam crawled up onto the bed and forced Nic to scoot back, never letting go of the tie. Cam's smirk turned positively wicked. "I'm glad you put this back on for me."

Falling back onto the pillows, Nic gazed at his husband through heavy-lidded eyes as he wound the tie through his fingers. Grew harder with each tiny jerk the motion caused. Nic wanted to feel those deft fingers on his cock. "Please, Boston. I held up my end of the deal."

"Time for me to hold up mine, then."

Cam let go of the tie end, grabbed a bottle of lube from the side table, and pushed Nic's thighs apart, almost painfully wide, but the warmth the exposed position brought to Nic's heart—the trust and openness there between them—was so much greater. And the pleasure when Cam's lips brushed his cock, featherlight, as his teeth tugged at the knotted tie was out of this world. Nic clutched the bedsheets, writhing and cursing, only making the exquisite torture worse. "Fucking hell."

"Almost got it."

Spoken words brought more lip contact, and Nic scrunched his eyes closed, fighting an orgasm that was right there. Cam's fingers against his hole, cool and slick with lube, didn't slow things down. Pressure assaulted him from both points of pleasure—insistent tugs and touches against his dick, thick fingers pushing into his ass. It was a sensory overload like Nic had never experienced. Two and a half years together and Cam could still blow his mind. He could only imagine what else they could get up to in the years to come. He babbled out his thanks, his praise, his love, ending on a roughened sigh when the pressure around his cock eased.

"Success!" Cam mumbled around—Nic opened his eyes again—the tie between his teeth.

"Impressive," Nic complimented. "But I don't think you can claim success until you get your dick inside me."

Cam cast aside the tie and stared down at him with dark eyes as heated as Nic was sure his own were. "Oh, is that the measure of success?"

"Tonight it is." Nic wound his legs around the backs of Cam's thighs and urged him forward. "I want my husband to make love to me."

Cam's devious grin softened, morphing into something soft and so full of love, an expression Nic could happily spend the rest of his life gazing up at. "There's nothing your husband wants to do more."

He didn't make either of them wait any longer, lining up and thrusting inside Nic. Hard, just the way Nic liked it, and fuck if Nic didn't love that feeling even more now that he wore a ring to match Cam's. He clawed at Cam's back and hitched his legs higher, bringing them chest to chest. Their sweat-slick bodies ground together as Cam pounded inside him, racing toward their climax. There was no more taking it slow. They'd teased enough already and had half a night—a lifetime— ahead of them for more of that. Now, though, was about releasing the desire that had built all day, about the love between them driving them higher. Faster. Until Cam stiffened in his arms and let out a deep, satisfied groan that unlocked Nic's own orgasm, the two of them coming together.

Cam collapsed first onto his elbows, then, with a nudge from Nic, completely on top of him. He shifted as if to slide off to Nic's side, but Nic tightened his legs around him, keeping Cam firmly in place. With his left hand, Nic reached over and grabbed Cam's, the metal of their rings pinging. Nic held them together, over his heart. "Couple of vows I forgot."

Cam propped his chin on their joined hands. "Oh yeah, what are those?"

"Do you promise to always argue with me?"

Cam grinned. "I do."

"To tell me if my beer sucks?"

Grinned bigger. "I do."

"To not give me too much shit for being a Kings fan?"

Laughed out loud. "I'll try."

Nic chuckled. "Fair enough."

Cam kissed his knuckles. "Got a few more of my own too."

"Figured you might."

Cam's grin morphed into a smirk. "Do you promise to always bring me donuts?"

An easy one. "I do."

"To always keep beer in the fridge and coffee ready to brew?"

Another easy one. "I do."

"To accept the fact you married a Southie boy who loves his Boston sports teams?"

Accepting Cam was the easy part—the easiest, best thing Nic had ever done—but the sports teams . . . "I'll try." He silenced Cam's dramatic guffaw by hauling him up for a kiss. "I love you, Cameron Byrne. Boston sports teams notwithstanding."

"And I love you, Dominic Price, including all that fancy legalese."

Their smiling lips met, sharing each other's breath, happiness, and bodies again and again, slow and teasing mixed with fast and rough, making the most of their wedding night.

Which remained blissfully uninterrupted.

Thank fuck.

GRAVITY CRAFT BREWERY
REDWOOD CITY, CA · EST. 2013
FIGHTING BOSTON IRISH
— IMPERIAL STOUT —
TROUBLE BREWING & LAYLAREYNE.COM

DANCE WITH ME

September 2021
(After Final Gravity)

Fittingly, it was another year before the stars aligned for a honeymoon. On their anniversary. And the only reason it happened then was because Lauren had blocked the days off in his and Cam's calendars as soon as the new year had rolled over.

Nic had half expected her to present them with an itinerary too, but it had been Cam who'd eagerly volunteered to plan everything, and Nic had happily relinquished all decision-making on the topic.

As the US Attorney for the Northern District of California now, he had more than enough of those to make on a daily basis.

Today, however, he was just a husband along for the ride.

But as Cam continued to drive their truck south along Highway 101, ever closer to where their lives had nearly been upended almost three years ago, Nic was beginning to question his decision not to participate in this particular decision.

He held his tongue, though, trusting his husband more than anyone else in the world. Until Cam took the freeway exit for the same state road that led to the coastal town where Duncan Vaughn's estate used to be.

He opened his mouth to question, but Cam's hand on his thigh, squeezing gently, forestalled him. "Trust me," he said.

Ten minutes later, Cam turned off the main road onto a gravel one that snaked through row after row of vineyards splashed in fall colors. Reds, yellows, and oranges, as far as Nic could see. "It's gorgeous."

"I thought the same when we were here last time. They're vines, but the colors still remind me of fall back east. I wanted to bring you back here to enjoy it when we weren't being chased or shot at."

Nic covered his hand and averted his gaze out the passenger window, blinking away the moisture in his eyes. From almost losing it all the last time they were here to having it all now as husbands. "It's perfect."

Before long, they came upon a compound of Spanish-style winery buildings, their adobe walls a warm buttery shade and the tile roofs glowing red in the evening sun. Cam drove right past them, following the narrowing road over several gently rolling hills of vines until a smaller structure, similar in style to the others, appeared atop the next hill.

It looked . . . peaceful. Not a word he associated often with their busy lives, but in moments like this, he realized how much they also needed it. A break from the chaos—and the casita that Cam parked the car in front looked like exactly that.

"Boston, this is perfect."

Cam waggled his brows, the dark eyes beneath them twinkling. "You haven't even seen the best part yet."

Which wasn't the open and airy living room with its soaring ceilings, oversize furniture, stone hearth, and sun-warmed floors.

Which also wasn't the spacious primary suite with its king-size bed, colorful quilts, and clawfoot table.

Which wasn't even the Jamie-worthy gourmet kitchen and overflowing baskets of fresh-baked breads and seasonal fruits that waited for them on the island.

"*This* is the best part," Cam said, holding open the back door for him.

Nic stepped into what could only be described as the most romantic setting of his life.

Fairy lights were strung along a vine-covered trellis, a stone fountain beside it gently gurgled, and a candlelit table for two, complete with a bottle of wine and glasses, set perched on a lookout over the hills of vines that were aglow with the evening sun.

Cam snaked his arms around him from behind. "Happy anniversary, baby."

"This is incredible." Beauty everywhere Nic looked, everywhere around him, including the man holding him in his arms. "I can't believe you did this."

"Give me some fucking credit." He playfully nipped the crook of his neck, then rested his chin on his shoulder. "I looked online through all the vineyards I could find around here. I liked this one best. Glad it lived up to the pictures." He shimmied his hips behind him. "Nice and private too."

That fact had also not escaped Nic. "Are we here the whole week?"

"The whole week."

Nic tipped back his head and angled his face, nuzzling the side of Cam's. "A whole fucking week." A proper vacation, in a beautiful, peaceful, private place, with his favorite person on Earth.

Whose hands were coasting lower, no doubt aiming to take advantage of said privacy. Before Cam reached his destination, Nic turned in his arms, then laughingly kissed his pout away. "We'll get there," he promised. "Every night this week. But there's something else I want to do with you first." Taking Cam by the hand, he led him under the trellis and into his arms. "Dance with me."

Smile as affectionate as Nic felt, Cam wound his arms around him and brought them cheek to cheek as they swayed to the music of the breeze rustling through the vineyards. "I can't think of a better way to celebrate the victory of us."

"Me neither." Nic brushed his lips over his husband's. "Happy anniversary, Boston."

THIS IS ME

June 2023
(During Best Play - Perfect Play 3.5)

Cam fought through the crowd of friends gathered around the bar and leaned his forearms on the bar top, narrowing his eyes at his husband. "You've been holding out on me."

Nic's smirk as he popped open bottles of Gravity's FBI Stout was the same one he'd been wearing all day.

As he'd strutted out of Aidan and Jamie's guest room in a pink fringe vest, tattered skinny jeans, rainbow-glitter cuffs, and combat boots to match.

As he'd strutted from the Embarcadero to the Civic Center, the very out and proud US Attorney for the Northern District of California at the helm of San Francisco's Pride Parade.

As he'd strutted behind the bar at Under the Table, case of beer over his shoulder, seemingly the master of ceremonies in this crowded corner of the Pride-themed bachelor party for their friends, Marsh and Levi.

That had been the first of six cases. Cam had been counting. Gravity's imperial stout was his favorite, his namesake one especially, and by his count, and by the number of red ale and pilsner pints multiplying around him, the stout should have been polished off a while ago. And yet, his husband had just made a "Last call on the imperial stout" shout from behind the bar.

Something didn't add up, and Cam—the trained investigator, stout enthusiast, and turned-on husband—was determined to find out what was going on. "Let's start with the beer," he said. "Where were you hiding the extra stout? Same place you were hiding that outfit?"

Heat danced in Nic's icy blue eyes. "That sounded like two questions."

"Answer them, Counselor."

He finished handing out bottles first, then grabbed the two bottles he'd reserved and slipped around to the front of the bar. "Feb tapped into her supply," he said as he handed Cam a bottle.

Nice of Jax's girlfriend who owned the joint. But that only answered one of Cam's questions.

"And the outfit?"

When Nic first appeared in it that morning, Cam had had to rush behind the kitchen island to hide his hard-on. Nic was turn-him-on-sexy any day, either in worn Levis and Gravity tees or one of his sharp, tailored suits. But dressed like he was today, with his tattoos visible beneath the vest and his long legs and fine ass poured into ripped jeans, Nic had been the source of Cam's temptation and thinning resistance all day long.

Made even more thin as Nic tipped back his beer and took several long swallows, his Adam's apple bobbing. He lowered the bottle and licked his lips. The fucker.

"Katie made me these," he said, showing off one of the sparkly bracelets. "Bought the rest when I was out with Lette one day for lunch." Nic's sister had never passed a vintage store she didn't wander into. "Saved it for a special occasion."

Cam gestured around them. "A bachelor party?"

Elbows propped on the bar, Nic leaned back and surveyed the crowd, and for a moment, Cam thought he was going to answer *yes*. But then he slowly returned his gaze to him and the earlier heat in his eyes had morphed into a determined fire, the same one Cam was used to seeing whenever Nic walked into a courtroom. And when he spoke, his voice carried the same intensity. "No, Boston, not a bachelor party."

All business, full of confidence, bordering on smug even. An attractive sort of arrogance that had driven every one of Nic's struts and smirks today. *Fuck you* energy, if Cam had to put a name to it.

A memory wire tripped. Nic and Eddie dismantling Duncan Vaughn's muscle in two seconds flat. They'd been full of the same sort of energy that night—and making a statement.

Like Nic was doing today.

"You're making a statement."

Nic tipped his head, a subtle acknowledgment, then finished his beer and set the empty on the bar behind him.

"Why now?" Cam asked.

"Things are changing," he answered. "I don't know what the world and this country are going to look like this time next year, or the year after that."

Cam felt it too. Saw it in the uptick of hate and anger that motivated an increasing number of cases that came across his desk. Even more reason to grab on to the good. He set his own empty aside, then moved in front of Nic, sliding his hands under the ends of his vest and splaying his fingers over warm inked skin. "So, we celebrate the victories while we still can."

"The victories and who we are. And this is me." He spread his arms wide, nothing to hide. "Dominic Price. Former SEAL and JAG captain. US Attorney with the highest close rate in the country. Brewery owner. Brother of Nicolette Sare. Husband of Cameron Patrick Byrne." He draped his arms over Cam's shoulders. "Who I married despite his horrible taste in sports teams."

"Says the Kings fan."

"Hey! We had a winning record this season."

Cam rolled his eyes. "Barely."

Nic grinned and erased the remaining distance between them, his warm breath drifting over Cam's lips. "I wanted to be real today. To be my whole self with my family and friends while I still could."

Cam groaned and buried his face in Nic's shoulder.

The rumble of laughter beneath his ear and against his chest was as sexy as the fucking outfit. "Got a problem with that, Boston?"

"Yeah," he mumbled before lifting his face enough to meet Nic's amused gaze. "You're not just unfairly good, you're unfairly perfect."

"I'm not perfect."

Cam begged to differ. He coasted his hands over Nic's hips and down, squeezing two handfuls of denim-clad ass cheeks. "Your butt is perfect in these jeans." Glided them back around and up Nic's torso, fingers raking through brown and silver chest hair and over the myriad of memories tattooed on Nic's skin. "Your inked chest in this vest." Continued to trace the ends of his tattoos over his shoulders and down his arms. "Every muscle between the fringe and the bracelets."

The shiver that rolled through Nic was a victory. The erection pressing against Cam's thigh too, as was the gravel in Nic's voice as he whispered, "If I was perfect, I wouldn't be mentally calculating how fast I can get you into a bathroom and get your mouth around my dick."

Cam's breath caught, then raced—right along with his heart and all of his blood rushing south. "That's exactly why you're perfect." He tangled his fingers with Nic's. "Ninety seconds," he added, before turning out of Nic's arms and tugging him into the crowd.

And into a blessedly empty bathroom a minute and a half later.

Another ninety seconds after that, he had Nic on the vanity cabinet in nothing but his fringe vest, his legs thrown over Cam's shoulders and his cock in his mouth.

"Fuck, yes," Nic cursed, as he clutched at Cam's rainbow-tipped hair. "I have been hard for this all day." He rocked his hips, filling Cam's mouth, his cock swelling with each thrust. "The hair, the eyeliner, that fucking jacket, that fucking shirt." Cam had recalled how much his Brady Campbell undercover ensemble had turned Nic on, so today he'd dressed for the occasion too, with an added *Bi and Badass* tee. "You talk about my jeans," Nic panted. "Every time you bent over I could see your bare ass through the tears in yours."

Cam drew back, an aching mess himself. "Stop trying to win the argument and come so I can get my dick in you."

Nic threw his head back on a groan, and fuck if Cam didn't wish he had a camera right then to capture the image. Sweat glistening on his man's heaving chest, precome dripping from his erect cock, all of his lean muscles, from his calves to his jaw, taut with tension.

Fucking perfect.

He glided his hands up Nic's thighs and clasped his hips, fingers splayed over the tattoos inked on each. "You're real, baby, and sexy as hell in a suit or in nothing but a pink fringe vest."

Nic righted his head, heat and devotion blazing in his heavy-lidded eyes. "You help me be me, and I love you for it." He laid a hand over Cam's on his left hip, over the clover with the stylized B there. "Now, being real . . ." he said, and added a smirk. "Make me come."

Ninety seconds after that, Nic was exploding in Cam's mouth, and a respectable several ninety seconds later, Cam ruined the pink fringe vest when we came all over his husband.

I GO WHERE HE GOES

October 2025
(After Angel's Share - Agents Irish & Whiskey 5)

It was bound to happen. Nic was honestly surprised it had taken this long. That Justice, under its current leadership, hadn't already found—or fabricated—a reason to get rid of him.

Aidan shifted forward in the chair beside him, resting his forearms on the table in Holding Room Two. "Did anyone actually see Attorney Price assault you?" he asked the visiting Assistant US Attorney across from them.

"A conference room full of agents and attorneys."

"And yet," Cam said from Nic's other side, "none of them have come forward to offer statements on your behalf."

"Conversely," Aidan continued, "we do have statements from those same people that you were screaming in a subordinate's face and that when you moved in a threatening manner toward her, Attorney Price intervened."

"He slammed me to the ground!" the AUSA whined.

"Hardly," Executive Assistant Director Moore scoffed behind them. "He tactically incapacitated you before you ended your own career by assaulting a fellow employee. He did you a favor."

"If Attorney Price had intended to *slam you to the ground,*" Aidan said, the impression so uncanny that Nic was reminded again of the SAC's past undercover exploits, "you'd be in the hospital and not sitting across from us."

The Associate Attorney General mediating this dispute, which had broken out over how hard to press a witness in what could only be described as a political prosecution that Nic wanted nothing to do with, shifted in his chair toward the AUSA—aka Asshole Attorney in Nic's head. Before the Associate AG could speak, though, their visitor withdrew a photo from his briefcase and tossed it onto the table.

Pictured was Nic at the San Francisco Pride Parade two years ago, dressed in his pink fridge vest and skinny jeans, hand in hand with his husband in his *Bi and Badass* tee and ripped jeans with his rainbow-tipped hair.

Beside him, Cam stiffened, and Nic was angry that the bigoted asshole across from them was taking one of the best days of his life, of his and Cam's marriage, and using it against them. What Nic wasn't, though, was embarrassed or the least bit chastened. He laid a hand on Cam's thigh and infused his voice with all the pride he'd felt that day. "That's me and my husband."

"*This*"—the AUSA poked violently at the photo—"violates the department's code of conduct."

Nic was tempted to reply *which part?* but settled for, "It didn't then."

"Do you pledge to never do it again?"

"Absolutely not. That"—he said with a nod at the picture

he wanted to steal and frame—"is me exercising my First Amendment rights."

"Look, Nic," the Associate AG said. "These are serious charges."

"Potential charges," Aidan corrected.

"Trumped-up ones," Cam muttered, and Nic suspected he meant in all the ways. "God forbid your best US Attorney be gay."

"Or a proponent of the First Amendment," Aidan added.

"Or victims' rights," El chimed in.

"Resign," the AUSA snapped. "Resign, and I won't press charges."

And there it was, the inevitable Nic had seen coming.

But unlike other upheavals in his life, this one wasn't accompanied by dryness in his mouth or heat prickling his skin. Instead, a wave of sorrow crashed over him—for the unraveling of the fabric of justice, the dismantling of the ideals he'd given thirty-plus years of his life for, as a soldier, a JAG, then a federal prosecutor.

Then, on the other side of that cresting wave of sadness was relief. The chance to get out from under a regime, an agenda so at odds with everything he stood for. To do something to fight against the further unraveling of the rule of law he'd sworn to uphold and of the country and its people he'd spent his entire adult life protecting.

"Is VERA still on the table?" he asked.

Technically, the voluntary early retirement program had closed months ago, but Nic was sure Asshole Attorney was connected enough—and wanted him gone enough—to make it happen.

Sure enough. "One day only. Take it or leave it."

"You can make that happen?"

A few texts later, the AUSA slid his phone across the table.

"It's done," he said as Nic read the confirmation himself. "You and any of your ilk," he added with a sneer directed at Aidan and Cam on either side of him.

"I've got it on tape," Lauren said through the comm in Nic's ear, and Nic glanced at the Associate AG, who nodded, giving his confirmation as well.

Nic bit back his threatening smirk as he held out a hand to Cam, who withdrew several sheets of folded paper from his coat pocket. He handed the first to Nic.

"My letter of resignation," Nic said as he flattened and pushed it across the table. The AUSA's victorious smile only lasted as long as it took Nic to lay the second sheet of paper on the table. "If you ever pay those benefits out, this is where they should go."

"The Talley Foundation? What kind of bullshit is this?"

"I am an immigrant," Aidan said as he placed his own letter of resignation atop Nic's and unfurled his full Irish accent. "My family immigrated here to escape domestic terrorists and religious zealots. I am done watching and aiding your cruel and illegal campaign to use those same tactics against our country and the people in it. I've still got a law degree. I'm going to put it to better use protecting our democracy and everyone in it."

El reached over Aidan's shoulder, gold band with its etched grape leaves twinkling on his ring finger, and added his resignation letter to the pile. "I couldn't agree more, which is why I've agreed to serve as the Foundation's executive director." He loosed his gleaming politician's smile. "This 'DEI hire' will see you on the Hill, lobbying for the people."

"And you?" Asshole Attorney sniped at Cam.

Leaning forward, Cam laid his resignation on the stack, then rested back in his chair, stretching one arm behind Nic and crossing the other in front of him to clasp Nic's hand. "I go where he goes."

A snide *this is what real partnership looks like* was on the tip of Nic's tongue, but the words were stolen by the lump in his throat that formed when the door opened, and a line of attorneys and agents passed through to lay their letters atop his and Cam's.

The lump grew bigger as Lauren added her resignation to the stack and moved to stand beside El behind him, followed by Marsh and Levi, SAC Kwan, Matty fucking Kim, Jazz Hands, and Farmer, and from the other coast, Charlotte Henby, another friend and the Bureau's star organized crime SAC. She was at the top of her game, as were all these attorneys and agents, his friends and family, his community, who were making a stand with him.

Whose names he would ink on his skin like he had his SEAL teammates who hadn't left him behind.

Jamie was the last of his family to crowd into the packed room. He had no resignation to give, years retired from the FBI, but the former baller and current coach brought juice of a different kind. "And I'll be making very public matching donations to the Foundation." He lowered himself into Aidan's lap, and the simmering outrage on the AUSA's face dissolved the lump in Nic's throat, his laughter bubbling up and out.

Outrage boiled over. "This is un-Amer—"

"I'm gonna stop you right there," Marsh drawled in his deep Texas accent. "Everyone in this room has served their country, and many of us are decorated military veterans, including Attorney Price."

"This wasn't what I intended."

"Funny thing that with your lot," Nic said as he leaned

more fully into Cam's side. "You never think about the long game."

"You can't do this."

"You want to go to war with us?" came Mel's voice from the doorway, her shoulder leaned against the jamb, and Nic mentally thanked her for getting all their friends and family here in such short order.

"You planned this," the AUSA seethed.

"Yes," Nic said. "Because I was the best US Attorney that Justice had, and I *did* think of the long game. I knew it was only a matter of time before you went after one of us."

"And if one of us goes," Aidan said, "we all go."

"We were ready," Cam agreed as he bumped his free fist against Jamie's.

From over Cam's shoulder, Matt slung a business card the AUSA's direction, hitting the asshole square in the forehead. It landed on the table, face up: *Rook Private Security.* "They're protected, if you and your boss even think of pulling some wannabe mobster bullshit. I'm from New York and worked in Boston. I know how real gangsters—and grifters—work."

"And if that doesn't convince you . . ." came the icy sharp voice of Hawes Madigan from beside Mel in the doorway.

He didn't need to say more.

Asshole Attorney paled, and the Associate AG quickly rose, knowing the game was up. "I believe we're done here."

With his friends and family at his back, his husband by his side, Nic's heart was full of love and pride, his soul filled with relief and purpose. He finally let his smirk loose.

"On the contrary—we're just getting started."

GRAVITY CRAFT BREWERY
REDWOOD CITY, CA · EST · 2013
TROUBLE BREWING · LAYLAREYNE.COM

ALSO BY LAYLA REYNE

For the most up-to-date list of titles and a helpful reading order, please visit www.laylareyne.com.

Agents Irish and Whiskey:

Single Malt

Cask Strength

Barrel Proof

Tequila Sunrise

Blended Whiskey

Angel's Share

Trouble Brewing:

Imperial Stout

Craft Brew

Noble Hops

Final Gravity

Fog City:

Prince of Killers

King Slayer

A New Empire

Queen's Ransom

Silent Knight

What We May Be

Perfect Play:

Dead Draw

Bad Bishop

King Hunt

Best Play

Redemption Inc:

The Accidental

The Bounty

The Martyr

The Boss

Guard Duty:

High Winds

Rough Waters

Wild Type:

Variable Onset

Affinity Drift

Matched Pair

Soul to Find:

Icarus and the Devil

Jason and the Storm

Paris and the Reaper

Atlas and the Traitor

Table for Two:

The Last Drop

Dine With Me

Blue Plate Special

Over a Barrel

The Sweet Spot

Sigh of Relief

Changing Lanes:

Relay

Medley

Freestyle

Three Sticks:

Barn Burner

Dirty Dangle

ABOUT THE AUTHOR

Layla Reyne is the author of *What We May Be* and the *Agents Irish and Whiskey*, *Fog City*, and *Perfect Play* series. She writes sexy, intense LGBTQIA+ romance featuring competent adults in kitchens, sports arenas, car chases, and other high-stakes situations. Whether it's adrenaline-fueled suspense, rival athletes, vampires and shifters, or love mixed with mouth-watering foodie goodness, queer folks finding happily-ever-afters is guaranteed.

You can find Layla online at laylareyne.com and at the following sites:

bookbub.com/authors/layla-reyne

facebook.com/laylareyne

instagram.com/laylareyne

tiktok.com/@laylareyne

bsky.app/profile/laylareyne

www.ingramcontent.com/pod-product-compliance
Lightning Source LLC
Chambersburg PA
CBHW071439300726
48976CB00004B/1385